One day as I was dreaming
Of sun and sand and sea...

Dido, my Darling

First published 2002 by Walker Books Ltd
87 Vauxhall Walk, London SE11 5HJ

2 4 6 8 10 9 7 5 3 1

© 2002 Camilla Ashforth

This book has been typeset in Columbus.
The pictures were done in watercolour and pencil.

Printed in Italy

British Library Cataloguing in Publication Data:
a catalogue record for this book is
available from the British Library

ISBN 0-7445-7565-6

WILLOW

by the Sea

Camilla Ashforth

WALKER BOOKS

AND SUBSIDIARIES

LONDON • BOSTON • SYDNEY

Whenever Willow wants to dream
he sits on his swing by the river.

From there he can gaze across Paradise Fields
and up to the Appleby Downs.

PARADISE FARM

One morning Willow sat dreaming
of the sea beyond the Downs.
He dreamt of the sound of waves
on the shore and Salt Cottage,
his house in the dunes.

All day long,
as Willow worked,
he thought of a trip
to the sea.

I really must take
Little Pig Pink …

and the horse
and the sheep …

and the cows.

The chickens and geese
will love it there.

So Willow
invited them all.

Next day Little Pig Pink helped Willow
pack the food for their trip.

Then they gathered the animals by
the gate and all set off for the sea.

As they made their way over the Appleby Downs,
Willow sang a song:

> One day as I was dreaming
> Of sun and sand and sea,
> I saw beyond the high hills
> A cottage made for me;
> A wind upon the water,
> A warm and wistful day,
> And miles and miles of sandy beach
> Where all of us will play
> Where all of us will play.

Beyond the Downs the animals stopped.

Ahead lay the beautiful sea.

They followed the path down to the shore.

Willow ran on to Salt Cottage.

He opened the door
and stepped inside.

SALT COTTAGE

It was just as he remembered.

Out on the beach the horse chased waves.

The chickens and geese played in the sand.

The sheep chewed on the salty grass.

The cows gazed into rock pools.

Willow came out to play on the beach.
Little Pig Pink was waiting.

Together they made
a mighty castle.

Together they splashed
in the waves.

"Let's play together for ever and ever," said Willow.
Little Pig Pink said, "Oink."

At tea-time the animals ate their picnic.

Carrots and corn and heaps of hay.

Oatcakes and apples for all.

Then side by side they sat on the sand
and watched the sun set before them.

Here we are together
Upon a golden shore
With setting sun and sand and sea,
As I dreamt before.
The warm wind's blowing cool now,
The sun is sinking low;
Our perfect day is ending
And so to bed we'll go
And so to bed we'll go.

"We all should sleep now," Willow said.
He settled the animals in the boat shed.

THE BOAT SHED

"You and I will sleep in Salt Cottage,"
whispered Willow to Little Pig Pink.

Willow kissed Little Pig Pink goodnight,
then he lay back on his pillow.

Lullaby boats are sailing
From far and distant lands
To scatter their catch of sweet dreams
Upon our silver sand
Upon our silver sand.

Willow's Sea Song

One day as I was dream - ing Of sun and sand and sea, _____ I
saw be - yond the high hills A cot - tage made for me; _____ A
wind up - on the wat - er, A warm and wist - ful day, _____ And
miles and miles of sand - y beach Where all of us will play. _____